Emergency Anthems

Alex Green

Further Praise for *Emergency Anthems*

"Anyone who knows his music writing knows that Alex Green knows music, and in this, his first book of poems, he seems also to know how to make it. Green's feel for the wheel—not to mention his insistence on keeping the moving parts clean—offers the reader a usefully clarified ride through the various terrains we live in and for; a grand (but never grandiose) tour of both world and word as they give sadly beautiful rise to one another..."

—Graham Foust, author of *In Time's Rift*

"In these strange and unnerving and very funny shorts, Alex Green conjures a drowning world where time moves like a moment of a thousand years and you will always be someone small on a stupid red bike. Comic, tender, realistic, and absurd, the stories introduce a cast of curious California characters: the Juilliard graduate who plays a lifeguard on TV and wants to make his character complicated but there's only so much he can do with scenes in a hot tub; the model who's struck by lightening and gets really good at yoga; a spider with muscles like an action figure, who opens a beetle like an egg. In this world, figs split open to reveal cities inside, the real problem is living too long, and the champagne you drink goes down cold and sharp like a 'world gone to glass, a decade turned to ice.' It's an astonishing world rendered in an astonishing voice. 'The world wheezes its secrets to a standstill and you stagger into her arms,' Green writes. I staggered into the arms of every single page."

—Marilyn Abildskov, author of *The Men In My Country*

"Alex Green's *Emergency Anthems* is the right kind of beautiful craziness for our times—a book of gorgeously written miniature narratives featuring magicians, musicians, actors, surfers, rabid bats, biting sharks, a missing astronaut, a deadly elevator, and a murderous rabbi. Together they make a summer-world of exuberance and tragedy, where the music rages until the tour bus flies off the freeway and the surfing is good until the sharks smell blood. Savor these stories one at a time or devour them all at once, but don't miss out."

—John Henry Fleming, author of *Songs For The Deaf*

Emergency Anthems

Alex Green

Brooklyn Arts Press · New York

Emergency Anthems
© 2014 Alex Green

ISBN-13: 978-1-936767-37-3

Cover design by Catherine Adams & Joe Pan. Interior by Joe Pan.

Published in the United States of America by:
Brooklyn Arts Press
154 N 9th St #1
Brooklyn, NY 11249
www.BrooklynArtsPress.com
info@BrooklynArtsPress.com

Distributed to the trade by Small Press Distribution (SPD)
www.spdbooks.org

Library of Congress Cataloging-in-Publication Data

Green, Alex.
  [Short stories. Selections]
  Emergency anthems / Alex Green.
      pages cm
  ISBN 978-1-936767-37-3 (pbk. : alk. paper)
  I. Title.

PS3607.R4297A6 2014
813'.6--dc23
                                    2014019662

First Edition; Second Printing

CONTENTS

II.

For Roland

From the otter pop summer to the Malibu shows, you remain the truest of friends.

Emergency Anthems

"It's never certain how these things will be carried on, but mysteriously it happens. Every night, somewhere on the outlaw side of some town, below some metaphysical 14th Street, out at the hard edges of some consensus about what's real, the continuity is always being sought, claimed, lost, found again, carried on."

—Thomas Pynchon, from the liner notes to Lotion's *Nobody's Cool*

"We know. Somehow we know when there's a shark around. It's a kind of sixth sense. I don't think we'll ever be able to document what it is exactly..."

—Peter Pyle, lecture to *Surfrider* members, San Francisco Chapter

ONE.

The Wide Gates of the Lowlands

The closing night of the campus production of *The Crucible*, you went to Cathy Hickman's party still in character: the long white wig, the tattered black poncho, the thick grey makeup that made you look hundreds of years old—from the moon and made of ashes. It was the same night they found the body of the sitar player in the hills above the golf course. For years he'd been performing midnight surgeries in a dark warehouse for anyone who wanted something done so much, it didn't matter if it was done terribly. When it was over, the patient would have to walk up the embankment and across the long empty parking lot, their body stinging with errors. Then the woozy ride home, the swerve in the stomach, the crude stitches weak with blood and losing their grip. They found him pretty much in pieces—dragged apart so far in the darkness, the police ran out of yellow tape at the crime scene. At the party you tried everything—you even did an impression of the puppet from that sitcom—but Cathy Hickman still wouldn't let you touch her. She sat far away from you on the couch and talked about waterskiing. And Italy. And a guy who was coming home from the Air Force. Later in your dorm room, you watched a metal band on TV play a concert in the Philippines. You stood in the bathroom and scraped the cakey makeup off your face while they played a song about burning Troy to the ground. The makeup fell away in big white clumps that collapsed under the hot water and dissolved in a long, grey stream. You looked in the mirror and were relieved to see that you were still young. It was the last time you would ever be that lucky.

Gene Clark

Gene Clark sunk your dad's boat off the coast of Regatta Del Mar. Your dad was so mad, you could hear him yelling a mile from the shore where you were surfing. His voice cut through the waves like something terrible and sharp. *I don't care who he is,* he screamed, *he owes me now.* But you were sure if your dad ever heard Gene Clark's voice roll under a tambourine or glide inside the jangle of a Rickenbacker, he'd change his mind and admit that it was he who owed Gene Clark something. The next day they met in your dad's office, and afterwards Gene Clark walked to the water, looking like he had been sad about the same thing since 1967. You followed him to the pier where he sat down on the edge; the boats of the cliff millionaires swayed together like royal swans and a plane dragged a chain across the sky. Gene Clark's hair hung in his face and he never looked up. A guy in a suit brought him something to drink and a stack of papers to sign. A blonde girl with an accent joined them and rubbed Gene Clark's shoulders. You could see yourself in the reflection of her hair; you memorized that species of light. At dusk the surfers walked in from the fading glow of the coastline. They left the beach in bursts of boards and electricity and, when they came back as silhouettes, that was when you were sure it would all end soon; that everything would sink and nothing—not even the crush of summer in Santa Monica—would ever matter again.

Dead Surfers and Distant Seconds

The rock climber loves the girl whose boyfriend was killed by a shark. But no matter what he does he'll always be in second place to the dead surfer who, in his last seconds, stumbled through the waves and back to the beach, blood surging from his side, just to say goodbye to her. Nothing can top that, but he keeps trying anyway. He tells her about sleeping on the side of a mountain, falling fifty feet into a jagged city of rocks, and how one time his knee exploded in so many pieces, the surgeons needed to bring in books to remember what it was supposed to look like. She tells him she's glad he's alive and falls asleep with her head on his chest in a way that feels patronizing. He feels his climbing scars glowing in embarrassment. No trial will ever be enough if later he's able to stand around at a party and say, *It was night, it was freezing, I had to hold my head together with a bungee cord.* But he knows the real problem is that he's lived too long. All he can do is imagine the dead boyfriend and the shark missing each other by miles. He pictures him walking unharmed from the water, sticking his board in the sand and lying down next to her. He says stupid things about the waves and the weather while she nods and reads a book about a blue wolf in an Arctic town. If only he had lived, he would have been powerless; and everyone else would have had a chance.

Last Broadcast, Avery Island

The band in the backyard busks behind the barbeque and the actor closes his eyes and wishes his birthday weren't over so soon. Next to him is his girlfriend, the one who wrote the article about how the heart has a seasonal migration, whether it wants one or not. Under the sunset, the patio and the pool turn to sepia and it's like watching a memory getting made. It's been that kind of a day. Years later it will end on the ski slopes and very badly. The ski patrol will look down the mountain and realize there's no point in hurrying. The actor's body will be loaded into the ambulance and the driver won't start the engine until he hears the last minute of a hockey game he doesn't even care about. These things will happen. But the girl will fall in love again; on ferries, outside cafés and across long kitchens in Hungary. She'll marry somebody, write articles about starting over and blah, blah, blah. The actor's last movie will finally be released years later. It's about the end of the world and it takes place mostly at night. In the final scene he lights something on fire and says, *Don't forget anything.*

Highlights from *Under the Sod*

In the novel *Under the Sod*, there are no characters in the first 338 pages. There's a great deal of vegetation, a few passages about the ocean, and a long chapter about fog. The first line of the fog chapter is, "The fog is the quietest species of weather," and the last line is, "One can be mauled in secret." Finally, there's the appearance of a painter wandering through a city plagued by such a terrible curse, it will never be lifted no matter how much somebody loves somebody else. For the next 654 pages the fog stops, the landscape gets considerably greener and people do things: a wrecked sailor with a bony compass for a heart wheezes against the boiling waves, a princess disguised as a sword maker cries into the fire, and in a tavern there's a fistfight between a playwright and another playwright. One of them thinks it's about the bill, the other thinks it's about a girl, but it's really about neither. The book then lapses into what critics have described as "deep pastoralia": boys chase girls through meadows, birds glide through laurel trees and a man stands on a hill overlooking the valley and plays a wood instrument that makes flowers open so wide, their petals arch their backs and snap off in mid-air. The next section is too long for most people; it's the kind of dense, slow-motion prose that makes you want to kill yourself. The 2,098 pages of this section can be best summarized in one sentence: "A man crawls on his stomach across the riverbank." In the book's final ten pages, there's a clash between two armies, it's night forever, nobody's happy, etc. The book ends at dusk, in a coat of half-light and shadows, the sky a layer of crimson, the horizon made of murder. Below the cliffs something opens and closes its jaws; a sailor with a fatal spider bite leans back and has to wait for weeks to never make it home.

Outside Tucker Luminar

You're not like your grandfather, who has kept every canceled check since 1937 in a fraying cardboard box that leaks a brown liquid when you move it. You write them and it's over. You throw away every love letter, you never look at old photographs, and you always give ten dollars to the guy on the street corner with the puppet. Inside your grandfather's bar, it always looks like Sunday afternoon. The bartender's arm has been in a sling for eight months; you help him by standing there and waiting for him to ask you to help him. Every morning you tear through the paper hoping to find that overnight the bar burned down. It doesn't matter how—an electrical accident, a sloppy suicide, a kid with matches—you just want to stand in the feathers of the foundation and lift the ashes into the air like a million dollars. But nothing ever changes. When you walk downtown everyone eats the same thing for lunch; men in suits try not to look like husbands, and behind you cell phones ring in relays of light jazz. Every day is the same. Your grandfather limps to the back office and pulls the shade; someone sobs over an old song on the jukebox from 1974 and the bartender reaches through his sling and pours. You have to get out of here.

California Divorce

At Makena beach on Maui, seven people are attacked by a shark in nine days. It could be all different sharks, but that's not the point. The point is they have only been married three days and now the honeymoon is ruined. She's sad about the places they could have gone, but she mourns Paris the most. *Honfleur, Gleyre,* she tells him. *Avignon, Bougival, L'Hôtel des Roches Noires.* He says he's only maybe heard of the last one. That night in the disco, she finally admits she doesn't think he's a good dancer. Later, when she sleeps, he thinks a lot about leaving. Six days later, they still haven't gone in the ocean. She watches a rerun of a sitcom from 1982 in Portuguese. He loses one thousand seventy-three dollars in a shell game to a guy in a hat whose hands move like chopper blades. In the afternoon they walk around the suite with their backs to each other. It's the kind of Sunday afternoon that makes you want to kill someone. Weeks later, swimmers slip back into the water, dogs chase tennis balls into the waves and at dusk surfers paddle in and dissolve on the beach, strumming acoustic guitars before twitching fires. Nobody knows for sure that the shark is gone; it's just a guess, a turn of the instinct that says, *Now.*

Summer Job, Year Seven

In California weathermen should get summers off, like teachers. The guy on channel 4 whose forecasts show suns in sunglasses drinking lemonade has started to annoy you. Coaching summer camp clinics at the tennis club, you have no mercy. Moody and vicious, you move the kids across the court until their faces turn to fevers. It's so hot, your heart puddles into a twitching black broil that burns through your shirt. At the end of the day angry-looking housewives pick up their kids in luxury cars, blasting air conditioners over easy rock from 1989. You stay stuck on Court 9, weary and fading, and feeding baskets of balls until it's finally dark enough to turn on the lights, which snap and click into a steady hum above you. In the parking lot the kid whose parents leave him there all day sits on the curb. He has learned to let nothing bother him. You have terrorized him all day with sprints and push-ups, but now he looks at you like he's never seen you before. He shows you five lizards he has caught and placed in a box lined with paper towels. He explains how he will put them back in the bushes, how they need to be treated as if nothing has happened. He crouches, placing them softly on the ground, whispers their temporary names with words of encouragement, and they disappear in camouflaged cursives into the darkness. It's not even July. You are going to be thirty-seven. It's the best thing you've seen in months.

Rescuer's Requiem

At the Olympics in London the swimmer who lived up the street stood on the blocks in a black suit and goggles. His body had rows of muscles like the kind you saw on the backs of jaguars in nature documentaries. It made you wish you had spent time getting great at something. Your city had stood still for him all summer: hardware stores and high schools were covered in banners, there were parades with marching bands and girls throwing batons through fire, and the coffee shop named a latte after him. You were supposed to want him to win, but before the race the profile of the guy from Belgium whose house had burned down was too compelling for you to take sides too quickly. His dad had fallen asleep smoking and the house went up in flames. Luckily everyone escaped. The clip ended with the swimmer and his father talking about healing and starting over, while passing a puppy between them. There were other stories, too: the Canadian whose bad heart was due to explode before he turned thirty; the Russian orphan who had witnessed a murder; the guy from France who was blind in one eye. But when they jumped from the blocks and started slicing through the water, you couldn't tell them apart—the Belgian with the burning house, the Canadian with the hourglass heart, the local Olympian who had gotten your sister and her best friend pregnant within a week of each other. You held your breath and felt stupid about the ways you planned to be famous: playing drums for The Young Murder Executives, escaping from handcuffs underwater surrounded by sharks, or stealing your brother's girlfriend, driving to another state, and writing a screenplay about how when you're madly in love, you'll destroy anyone. But suddenly all you wanted was to live through a horrible disaster and from your newly furnished apartment talk about starting over on national television. You wanted to stare into the interviewer's eyes and say, *After the explosion, I became the fastest man in the world.*

The Sky Wet with Signals

Even though he graduates from Juilliard with flash and promise, when the actor moves to L.A., he gets a part on a television series called "Malibu Silk" playing a lifeguard who rides a motorcycle late at night. He tries to make the character complicated and tragic, but there's only so much he can convey when most of the scenes take place in a hot tub. Frustrated, he takes control of the direction and in one scene, instead of kissing the Senator's daughter while sensual synth reggae plays, he stares up at the sky and delivers a monologue about dying in the rain. Shooting the scene takes most of the day. The real director could care less—he sits smoking in a chair with his headphones on, listening to an industrial band from Canada whose singer was killed in a bar over a disagreement about a girl he'd only known for two days. The director has rabies and is weak from the fifth round of shots; he's barely eaten in weeks and falls asleep at traffic lights. Like a low, dense fog, a flush has permanently settled upon him, making his clothes sticky all day. A bat had flown in his bedroom window and bit him on the arm before finding its way back into the night. *Do you still have the bat*, the vet asked. *I never had the bat*, the director said. *It'd be better if we had the bat*, said the vet. The shots turned his blood hot and thick; it makes him feel like something big and heaving that drags itself across swamps. When people ask him what's wrong, he's never be able to explain it right; no matter how many times he says, *Gothic fever, terrible moon, the sky wet with signals.*

Giverny Floodlands

Until the girl who called you in the middle of the night and said, *I have a fever because of this thing*, slides from the dark embers of your arms, you'll always be standing on the porch in the rain, listening to the bells of the university. Soon there will be an undergraduate with an oar that can slice water into obedient strips. Soon there will be a boy who can make all the girls turn colors. Somebody will borrow a boat one weekend and you'll never see her again. The press of the campus and all the deep semester voodoo makes you think there are too many things in your mouth. Soon it will really be winter; the frozen faculty will slowly move to meetings with the crooked shoulders of a Greek chorus, and out every window you'll study the lights of the freeway trying to spot a car crash. You can already hear the mix of metal scraping against the engine; the static of crushed speakers, the wild hiss of wires, the flickering signal in a city of radios.

While the Woods Were Burning

Bill Tilden didn't go to the tennis tournament in Australia. Because his shoulder was shattered, he smoked cigarettes in the backyard of the summer mansion and listened to phonograph records of sad songs played by big bands. He kept the volume low so it always sounded distant, like a girl crying on the 8th floor of a hotel, or the bells of a cathedral in the background of a scratchy phone call from Lyon. He felt too old for revenge, too broken to roam the late night cities of the world drinking black market cocktails and tripping down alleys holding someone else's knife. News of the Russian acrobats' caravan exploding in the forest reached him by butler in the twilight. In the wake of the grim reports he wondered if at least one of the unbreakable boys with springing limbs found his way through the flames, backflipped above the trees, and somersaulted to secret safety. *Great tragedy should always offer at least one splendid thing*, he thought, as he let the night pull him under its big dirty cape. His shoulder dug sharply into his skin, love turned back into smoke and the woods whistled with acrobats on fire.

Shadowing the Parasol

The woman the magician is supposed to love writes a book about the history of umbrellas called *Shadowing The Parasol*. When she reads at universities and bookstores, people have her sign their copies like she's some kind of sunshade rock star. The magician sits in the audience making coins disappear one after the other, not even bothering to pull them back from the slip in the air where he placed them. After seeing him perform, one critic wrote: *Watching everyone else now is like watching someone learn to play the guitar.* But he misses his days of being a young pickpocket, the simple flow of keys, the glide of leather wallets sailing into his jacket. He misses the intimacy of that brand of vandalism. He also misses being in late-semester love with the actress who spoke in long, clean sentences and sang in big bluesy notes that startled him into tenderness. Watching her perform would always make him feel generous: he'd imagine reaching his hand into the hovering world, bringing back things made of light, placing them into long, empty laps. She is the only thing he ever lost that he wasn't able to find again. While the writer answers umbrella questions about the palm leaves of Ancient Egypt and the feathers and gold of the Aztec Empire, he aches to be crooked and in love again. How pure it felt to walk the roads of the Northern town to her house like a thief, knowing that in the morning no one would be able to tell the difference between broken glass and ice.

A Person's Guide to the Rest of Summer

After your son is attacked by a shark, you sit in the waiting room of the hospital that overlooks the ocean and think: *This is what a vacation looks like when it's not working.* You can see the nurses' tan lines glowing under their uniforms. When they pass by they smell like suntan oil and summer in America. The one you've had your eye on comes over to you; she looks like the actress from the television show *F.B.I. Beach Patrol.* You remember one episode when she chased a bank robber down the beach and broke both his legs; the bills flew loose from the sack and went limp in the waves. The nurse tells you it's bad, but it's good your son is young. She explains the problems with the mouths of sharks and how the scar will stretch in a rickety seam down his side. After she leaves, you notice how the sand has hardened all over your body; when you move it cracks down your back and across your stomach. You spit in your palms to get rid of the chalky thickness. A surfer whose elbow splinters out of his bicep like a mangled umbrella sways back and forth in the seat next to you. Water from his hair sprays lightly on your cheek and you want to hold him like a healer, sail his bones into each other, let him loose back into the waves.

All Night the Airfields, Amy Winehouse

In the middle of the night, nothing you can't handle: a man at the end of an alley dragging an axe, a loneliness so vast it electrocutes the throat with the sting of awareness. But then the girl with lead in her hand slides next to you like a searchlight and your career of nights goes quiet; slips from the radar and cascades into the blue of abandoned fathoms. Summer is over in a swift and soundless mugging; the figs sit split open on the tree, their cities inside already turning to dust. It's an astonishing new season. The world wheezes its secrets to a standstill and you stagger into her arms.

The World and What to Do with It

At the end of the semester it still isn't winter; the trees, brown and folded, hang off the side of the hill like dead parachutists. Experts say there won't be clouds for weeks; the endless sheets of blue sky are predicted to never stop. It's warm, it's dry, and across the city, one by one, houses wrapped in Christmas lights catch fire. Some people walk around slow and stunned while others sit on the hoods of their broken down cars. Across the city no one is really sure if it's an emergency, so they stay on the beach, vibrating with volleyballs and radios and surfboards. And even though every now and then they get kind of nervous, worry can't last for long under such a winning streak of sun. You turn your grades in and catch your breath at the knees of the university. Later in an old sailboat you sit in the water and wait for anything resembling a breeze. On the radio the weatherman has resorted to shorthand and just says, *More of this*. You sprinkle ice into a glass, pour lemonade over it, and listen to its bones snap across the harbor. You remember a story about a spaceman who floated away and disappeared for weeks behind the moon. *I thought I was dead*, he said years later. *And I thought it was going to stay that way forever.*

West Coast Wreckage

The singer for the Young Murder Executives doesn't know how to break up with his girlfriend. He thinks about writing her a note or having a serious dinner with her under the soft lights of a restaurant by the water, but secretly wishes he could just disappear quietly with the actress from Spain. Looking around their apartment, he should be thinking, *This is what life looks like when you let the air out. This is a head start on the aftermath.* But instead he leans over the balcony and tries to read a book about something that happened in Turkey in 1923. Below he sees the surfing instructor talking to a girl. He stares at her reflection in the glare of the board—she's made of silver, she's outlined in italics, she looks like someone who's been alive forever. Down the promenade a guy juggles chainsaws and bowling balls and fiery torches. A kid with an acoustic guitar plays an old Irish song about boats and wars and the open hearts of the dead. He's not sure which of them makes him feel worse. While he waits for her to come home he watches a show on television about things in Australia that can kill you. A spider with the kind of muscles usually found on plastic action figures breaks open a beetle like an egg. It throbs in and out of the black shell until it eases into liquid.

American Stutter

But before that, the fog would come out of the mineral factory and below the dock in italics a boat swayed like perhaps, perhaps. And in your American stutter you lapse into the moment of a thousand years, where you are driving down a freeway toward the ocean, holding a phone against your glowing jaw and wearing sunglasses that airbrush everything into sepia footage from a '60s surf film. On the beach a couple holding hands runs toward the water, a surfer shines his board into a still-life, and you can't remember the name of the girl who drowned anymore. But you do remember how they churned through the water, pulling her from the choppy palace and turning her body in circles, like they were smothering a fire. And when they slid her suit halfway down her body, you felt the sunset on your shoulders break upon your back like decades. You stood behind the coast guard who had collapsed over her in measured sobs. Even though you were only a boy, you could feel her count to ten and kiss the air between his lips right before he gave up. The only other thing you remember is the radio on the drive home. There was a baseball game, then there wasn't. Then on the news a man whose house had disappeared in a flood told a reporter he was tired of talking about water.

Birthday Poem in B-Flat

The bees are back; they twitch and swell inside the hive and blare their blurry New Wave across the street. On Friday she is stung eight times and collapses on the grass. Smoke slips from the holes in her arms and legs and above you there is sizzling in the leaves. The next day you stand with the beekeeper's son and stare up at the hive; it throbs and breathes like an organ doing what it's supposed to do. He climbs up the tree in a netted mask, holding a metal stake with the elegance of a fencer. You can't help but notice the surgical way he guides it under the branches. Later the bees are gone, but nothing has changed. It's still summer, it's still June, you still hate your life so much you can taste it on the back of your throat. And in every dream the hive is bigger; in every dream, breathless against the branches, the beekeeper's son raises it to the sky, and it lifts him above the houses.

Coastal Clockwork

In a small seaside town the movie theater closes at 8:30, whether the movie is over or not.

Slow Motion Ballet

The gymnast watches the lightning from the window of the studio; it flashes against the sky like an unpronounceable consonant. It's only been 57 days, but already she notices a wobble in the gait of her marriage. She can't stop thinking about the boy in college who was killed in an elevator on his way up to her room on the tenth floor. In the dark they'd stumble across campus and sneak into the pool or step into the red fog of the hot tub and spend hours monstrous and lovely. But one night something loosened through the building and she could hear the snapping of gears, the cables whipping open, crushing him under a network of spikes. Later, the scene was lined with yellow tape, like the mouth of a mineshaft roped off after an accident. She remembers the saliva of sparking wires, hissing and whipping like mythical serpents and hanging loosely from the ceiling. Police and paramedics and electricians moved in and out of the wreckage in a slow-motion ballet. The girls on the floor clutched their bathrobes to their necks and cried when the boy's body came out, zipped safely behind blue vinyl. After that, the gymnast doesn't remember anything. Except the semester giving way to a summer of tilting skies. Except working as a lifeguard and spending her breaks driving her car in circles around the parking lot. Except the actor on the news standing in his underwear while his house burned down behind him. Through the television speakers the flames were muffled and distant, like the rare old stuff of a lullaby; like somebody's memory of how the ocean sounds.

South Marine Highway Love Song

In the middle of 279 hours of hard rain, there's a sinkhole in Santa Monica, a long throw of concrete and tar that arches its back and buckles, teeth spitting up rocks and broken pipes and other bones of the suburbs. You and your daughter sit in a café watching the workers with their cranes and lights try to wrap the great tongues of road back into the earth. When the waitress pours your tea, the strap of her bra slides to the left and you see the tan-line behind it. Your daughter draws a picture of a palm tree and under it a rabbit and a puppy. Above them she puts a sun with thick spikes of heat that hover in menacing bolts so close to the ground it would burn both of them in seconds. But instead of telling her this, you ask why the rabbit is blue. It's too late in the day for surprises; it's not going to stop raining and the waitress is not going to touch your shoulder and whisper *maybe* behind the soft hiss of hot water. You are on your own and you will have to make decisions about the world like you know what you're doing. Your daughter can't ever see you wither with doubt; can't ever see you wondering about the names of things. In the street the sinkhole keeps stacking layers to the sky; the workmen's failed geometry keeps it a tarry gash that will not close. Outside the café, a girl in a blue raincoat twirls an umbrella. Inside, the radio plays a song about wolves. Using a red crayon your daughter covers her drawing in great slashes of flames, explains that it's raining fire and everything is going to melt and there's nothing anyone can do. She is getting the idea.

Scene 4: Dim Lights

Down the path, serious as a former champion, Sunblast is smoldering and smoking a cigarette from Holland backwards to get his money's worth. The storm has been called off; something cold in the Pacific did some damage even the weatherman can't explain. In the dark you feel the ceiling start to leak again. The thing the guy at the hardware store sold you has loosened. You hear the water slide down the wall in fourths. The electric sand dollar is broken, lies drowned in mid-orange. The doorplate of the poet upstairs still says *Poet Upstairs* and the spinning boy hasn't spoken in years; keeps turning in circles in the middle of the plaza, like a fountain.

Strobe Light Retrospective

Nobody could believe the rabbi murdered his wife, but it was true. He drowned her in the big hot tub in their backyard, made a quiet phone call to the police, and waited for them out front. *These are the things we do as people*, he'd said. You were fourteen and didn't know rabbis killed their wives—you didn't know they had hot tubs, either. All summer at Temple you sat behind Sheyna Dumas and watched the tan lines brighten across her back. From shoulder to shoulder you imagined crossing that golden bridge. The new rabbi was young and tried to sound too cool; he talked a lot about baseball and quoted a rock band no one had liked in years. You only paid attention to the cantor who sang songs from a centerless alphabet. Listening to her voice climb and burst in triumphant triple axles made you feel swollen with promise and destiny. At night in your parents' pool you floated on your back and made up fake Yiddish constellations: Shlomo the magician, Harel the racquetball champion. The season was almost over; in the water you felt the heat fading beneath you. You stayed up late watching talk shows and nature documentaries. In one, a lost kit fox traveled the Arctic tundra alone for weeks. You cried when he made it home. Sometimes you imagined the rabbi small in his cell and pacing away the rest of his life, but not very often. You were about to start high school and had begun to think of Temple as a place where you used to go. All you could really think about was how in a few weeks you would be slow dancing with girls; how you would slowly step under the strobe light that splashed over the gym floor and follow the beaming circles of the dappled path, blinking in a trail in front of you.

Australian Divorce

Because you are so far behind, you decide to take your marriage
Pass/Fail. And then that's it. Sometimes you go to work, but
mostly you surf Eade Point, then sit on the beach and watch
people try to talk to each other. It won't get better but it doesn't
matter; by now you are used to the sharks that move under the
relay of radios; the slip of the surf in a summer of cheaters.

Why You'll Never Live in Ithaca

On the porch you tell a girl a stupid story about Easter and the fire you started in the kitchen by accident. It's a relief when bad things become funny. It's a relief when you can sit around a table with a group of friends and say, *The car just kept going over the cliff.* But it's terrible when you remember the chocolate rabbits melting in their boxes, the flames throwing open the cabinet doors, crawling under the floor and exploding under the refrigerator. On the eighth floor of a hotel she takes off her clothes and angles over you, and you want everything that's about to happen to stay that way: let the girl hover, let the stereo stay broken, let the music inside keep holding its breath.

Stereo Embers

In her house below the river she had five thousand records. The needle on her stereo was bad; it bent its knees and straightened, it broke over the vinyl in slow gasps. Every song she played carried the same fatigue. There was no television, you drank juice out of jars and while you slept she would keep trying to sketch your portrait, but each one ended up being a train stuck somewhere in the darkness. Every night you would pull her tank top off her shoulders, but you were so sick of being young, there wasn't anything you could do for her. After she moved without telling anybody, you watched the rangers smoking cigarettes at the edge of the woods and had the first terrible feeling that people are never who they say they are.

Why a Chokehold only Works if the Person Is Standing near You

On the news you never hear about someone who is good at karate saving the day; banks get robbed, cars get stolen, buildings explode, but no crime ever gets derailed by a black belt who can kick the air into stars and snap limbs behind his back. Once you signed up for a martial arts class, but in the first few minutes you tore your groin so badly you felt the muscle split from the bone and orbit violently below your abdomen. In the car, the pain vibrated in the new pocket of empty space. When you got home you needed the retired magician with emphysema to help you out of your car and into your house. You fell asleep on the couch to a cooking show in which everybody cheered when alcohol and cheese got added to pasta sauce. When you woke up, the magician was still there, sitting next to you and passing coins over his fingers; you watched the silver rise from nowhere, stand up like wheels, and roll down his wrists, moving to the beat of what little breath he had left. You could hear how the gears of his lungs had snapped and were gone—you imagined them wet and frayed, dangling over the boneless galaxies of his throat. There was dried blood on the wall, the lights kept flickering and you were sure you would never be amazed by anything ever again.

University Simmer

In college you played her The Stone Roses hoping that something would happen, but nothing did. She only wanted to talk about The Captain, who was away rockclimbing for the weekend. You told her everything you knew about him: his modeling career, the accident on the island and the robbery in Thailand. She said none of it sounded right except for the part about the modeling. She also said The Captain's policy seemed to be about always being a hundred miles away from anyone. You made a joke about that being true even if he was sitting right next to you. She didn't say anything back. After she left you watched a movie about a werewolf you had seen years before. You didn't remember it being so depressing. Down the hall the Bactoli brothers were beating someone else up and on the grass outside the dorm two actors were practicing a sequence with swords. They kept going even when the sprinklers started. From your window they looked like sketches of skeletons sparring in the moonlight.

Farewell to the Captain

By the time you got to the Captain, his car was almost packed and it was already raining. You can't remember if it was winter or what was left of it. Watching him put the rest of his things in the trunk—a surfboard, a crate of old records, a stuffed rabbit with a hand missing—you felt like you were still paying attention to all the wrong things about him.

TWO.

They'll Know When You're Gone

The people in the ad for the health club don't actually belong to the health club. The girl on the elliptical trainer is a singer from Portland who has written hundreds of songs about dead surfers. At night she stays awake listening to her hermit crab shift in his tank while imagining someone on the roof with a knife and a bad knee. The guy with the towel around his neck stars in movies about lifeguards and rock stars and people pretending to be rich and terrible in Malibu. He holds the record for most scenes shot in a hot tub (124) and most consecutive movies with the word "heat" in the title (9). The thing that troubles him most in the world is that he knows exactly how much time he has left to look carelessly handsome. The kids in the pool aren't related or even friends; in real life they eat candy the color of electricity, do sports that mostly bore them, and play video games about murder sprees in outer space. Not only are the couple in the sauna not married, the picture wasn't even shot with them in the same room. She does print work for clothing catalogues for an agency in Vermont, but her fake husband's shirtless picture was stolen from an ad in a European hospitality magazine and Photoshopped in to make it look like they were together. The real guy will never find this out. He'll continue to play a ski instructor on a German soap opera and his synth pop band, Klaberjass will do quite well. Their hit "Dance Ceramics" will stay atop the charts for a record number of weeks (34). A staggering number of people will fall in love to it on the dance floor (12,987). One of these couples will break up and the boy will take it very badly. He'll tell someone his heart feels like a house that has slid down a muddy riverbank and collapsed into the rapids. They won't know what to say. Years later he'll write an essay called "The Trouble with Love Is You Never Forget How You Thought You Felt." It will be published in an esteemed journal and the cover will be a drawing of a robot with a heart over its head offering a flower to a seal. The drawing will become very famous. It will make people feel terrible and hopeful. It will be called "It Doesn't Matter What Happens Next."

Sag Harbor Chanty

After the model is struck by lightning she becomes really good at yoga. She teaches classes at the small studio by the harbor and afterwards has long talks in the parking lot with her students. She sees the way they stare at her, like any minute something else might happen. And they all ask the same questions: they want to know if the current helped her bend better, or if she can feel things about the future. Sometimes she wishes the lightning had done what it was supposed to do, but she's never said this out loud. Her boyfriend makes jokes at parties about how the television reception is clearer now, or how he'll stand apart from her when they walk in the rain. Truthfully, she doesn't really like him very much anymore. In horror movies, skinny bolts in lightning storms walk across the sky with the shuddering legs of a yearling, but she knows that's not how it really is. She remembers how it pushed against the night and lit up the sky's nervous system before singling her out. In class a woman who was attacked by a shark shows her the scar that starts at her calf and gets wider as it winds up her waist. It's the first map of an emergency she has ever seen and she can't turn away. The frayed faultline is like a fossil of electricity, evidence of a fever. In it she recognizes the turn and rip of the current, the break of a bite from nowhere—

Solstice Studies

The bodybuilder was enormous. He'd stack plates on bars, pick them up, then put them down like a Stone Age hero. He never spoke and everyone stayed out of his way. But on the last day of summer, he pushed Steve Malthorp through a window and dangled him from the balcony with one hand. When they first came together the building shook and felt like it was cracking beneath you. Their quick grapple came as a suckerpunch of silence that made everyone stop what they were doing. You tried to watch but the sun through the window came at you too fast, like the thing that happens before a concussion. It was never really a contest and Malthorp, the Olympic wrestler, wide and full of storms, glided easily through the glass. From far away it looked slow and unreal, like the bodybuilder was reversing archeology and putting man back into ice. When he opened his hand, you sensed something casual and sharp coming from another season and you knew summer wouldn't last much longer. You squinted through the glare and watched Malthorp flip backwards and fall thirty feet into the end of August.

Breaker's Kaddish

In 1983 ten members of the Israeli wrestling team were killed when their driver slipped into a shallow sleep and their van jumped the overpass, fell twenty-eight feet, and sank into the ocean. Only Ziv Levy, who was sitting in the front seat, survived. He went through the windshield and landed safely on the sidewalk. He had known his teammates all his life. He had been to their Bar Mitzvahs, eaten endless meals with their parents, and had even kissed some of their sisters in high school. Lying on the asphalt, blood spilled from his mouth. Whenever he tried to move, something in his ribs kept crumbling into smaller bits. The bones of his wrists felt like boiling water. And yet he lived. It took months, but he came back stronger than ever. He spent every day lifting weights, jumping rope, and wrestling students from the university. He ate five meals a day, gorged on ancient grains and secret soups. He spoke as little as possible and slept with prostitutes. He felt depressed whenever he bought groceries. He longed for the days when a great chorus of laughter would leave him holding his side. Late one night, he walked to the beach. There he watched two harbor fishermen pull nets from the surf, disco blaring from a battered tape deck. He turned away and saw a boy and his girlfriend dancing on the sand to the music. The boy's shirt was unbuttoned and the girl wore a black dress. As they swung in slow motion she seemed to whisper into his ear, *Like this, like this.*

Why a Scar Is Better than Being Good at Swordfighting

The soccer player who was bitten by a shark has a scar that sits under his eye like a spiny fossil. He gets all the girls because it makes him look tough; they can see how violence failed on him, how it only managed to glide against his face in a weak splash. He kicks winning goals, he gets perfect grades, and to make matters worse, he's a really nice guy. He's kind and thoughtful and speaks quietly as if he's always discussing the delicate childhood of someone nearby. You make everyone laugh with impressions of your professors and your ventriloquist act with a sandwich, but that's about all you've got. You're old enough to understand that funny always loses to a scar. At night you stare in the mirror and think about giving yourself one, just to even things up. A quick swipe with a knife could mean years of girls, but you worry about how far to take the blade, or if the bleeding will stop on its own. You'd probably go too deep, puncture an artery; or you'd go too shallow for stitches and end up bandaged and embarrassed, known forever as a fraud. But the real problem is you wouldn't know how to live under a scar—how to act, how to stand, what to say when people ask about it. Instead you try to carve your initials in the wood frame above the window. As you slice away, the blade goes hot in your hand and the letters break in half on the grain.

David Naughton at Midnight, Full Moon, etc.

Shelly Beecher was so metal: pregnant in 9th grade, smoking on the grass behind the lockers in her Iron Maiden t-shirt. Her boyfriend, Tom Moody, was a senior, and he had muscles and a moustache and a car with no muffler that jackhammered across the parking lot every morning. One day in class you let her copy your *Great Expectations* quiz and after that you never saw her again. It didn't take long for Tom Moody to get a new girlfriend; she was blonde and wore dresses with skulls on them, and when they kissed against his locker, she'd put both hands on his face. You hoped she would destroy him quickly. The night the moon did something it does every three thousand years, all the members of a famous hard rock band were killed when their tour bus flew off the freeway and exploded in an empty field behind the miniature golf course. On the news, smoke tumbled from the twisted knots of scattered fuselage, and firemen ran relays with hoses around giant burning dragons. Paramedics knelt over bodies as policemen took notes and the cameraman trained his lens on a tennis shoe in the bushes. Behind the reporter, a girl in a bikini with wet black eyes emerged from a patch of smoking debris to wander in circles in the ash. A few hours later, while cleaning your parents' pool, you pulled a mouse from the drain and set it down in the grass. Crushed by the press of water, it gasped and steadied itself in the moonlight. You wanted it to dart back into the night but it didn't; it just stared straight ahead like it was waiting for you to do the same thing. You still can't remember who moved first.

Summer at Pitch 77

In late June at dusk, everyone was a silhouette playing with a dog on their lawn. But when the daughter of the doctor let the straps of her swimsuit fall off her shoulders, that's when the summer finally started. When you got in a fight with the kid across the street and he slashed your face with chickenwire, your dad gave you a sip of brandy, wrapped your head in gauze, and the two of you sat on the couch playing chess like a wounded Russian general and his trusty medic. You were too young to be a contender, but you wanted her to see you injured; you wanted to walk past her house the next day, bandaged like the street celebrity. But Jack Marobi, who played guitar on his driveway with a hazy smile under feathered hair, stole the spotlight when he got caught breaking into the sporting goods store and dedicated his crime to her on the evening news. Even though he ended up going to jail for seven months, you wished you had thought of it first. In July she worked for the Senator and later she'd go to that college in Massachusetts, never to come home again, even when her dad cured a terrible disease and television cameras lined up outside their house for two days. Before August ended you fell in love with Leslie Miley, who moved from Georgia and swam out back with your sister; thought maybe if you got hit by a car, there was an outside chance she might love you. When the nights grew shallow and school was ready to start again, you wondered if in his cell Jack Marobi knew the season was over; if he would lie in bed in the dark and listen to the sounds of summer turning to static.

West Coast Dub

On the back porch, fractured ska leaks from a broken speaker; the shadow of the roof on the pavement looks like the outline of California on a treasure map. At night in the windows of the gift shops, lamps in the shapes of dogs and houses are lit and glowing like weekends. Every time she leaves it feels like she's changing her mind. You try to be happy but nothing really works. You end up spending the rest of the night trying to spot the blue wolf that experts say moves low to the ground like a stingray. By dawn you've seen nothing. On the beach, a woman does Tai Chi in slow motion and a man who used to be a priest leans against his surfboard and smokes. The pier sways above the water like a calypso contrary; a shipwrecking of the eyes, the breath in the back of a net.

Karina around the Bend

And then July kicked into double overtime and the Danish girl who rolled the cliff millionaires' kids around the country club snuck you through the window of the Western Estate and taught you how to say *wolf*. In the daytime she'd sit by the pool, and you'd watch the tan settle on her skin like perfect reception. At night you'd sit together in your apartment talking about the next hundred years and you'd promise her you'd quit your job hitting tennis balls at unhappy housewives. She'd open the atlas and point to old European cities, tell stories of her father forcing metal together in the shipyard and her mother breaking her ankle ice skating in the 1960 Olympics. While she slept you imagined crouching in hollow horses in the shadows of cold embassies. And you planned on breaking into the furniture store, stealing couches and lamps and tables, strapping them on your back like a Dr. Seuss character and careening down a crooked hill to her, the mossy roofs of the village leaning over the houses in soggy shadows. Before people leave they say three things they don't mean and one thing they forgot to tell you that changes everything. She did all four at once. For the rest of the summer you sat in the dark alone, the fracture in your shoulder aching underneath your skin. You could feel the dim glow the doctor showed you on the X-ray stitching through the bone; it moved in a low, terrible hum under the covers.

Tillbrook Crimes

You play golf with your grandfather and his friends because it's his birthday, and their usual fourth—the lawyer from Browning, Abrahms, & The Other Guy—can't make it. You swing your club awkwardly, watch every ball hook off the course with the wrong kind of geometry. On the twelfth hole you follow your ball into the graveyard while the rest of them play on. In the grass a fox ties a stolen shoelace into a knot with his teeth. You skip the remaining holes to watch him stitch the ends together and think of more lies to tell your daughter. You'll say it was a mountain lion. You'll say your band was famous in Denmark in the '80s. You'll say you drove your car into the ocean on purpose. In the clubhouse your grandfather lights a cigar; smoke unravels from his mouth and bends upward in a smooth, skeletal stretch. To show how bad your shots were, one of the golfers turns his hands into triangles, raises them above his head and tilts to the side. It's like an excerpt from a dance that everyone but you knows. There is a toast. Your drink is thin, like a venom that can kill you and never be detected. You still haven't told anyone your wife is living with a soldier. Or that you sold your drum set. For the first time in your life you miss the post-game chatter of golf in the seventh grade. You and your friends would lean against lockers, and when the right girl walked by you'd say, *"Right in the middle. Right in the middle of the mouth of the dragon."*

Blue Door Option

Everybody knew the magician was dying and this would be his last party. All of his ex-girlfriends were there—even Stacey Mitchell, the news anchor who he had lived with on a houseboat in the '70s when he held his breath for the whole summer. Today he was taking requests. He would make birds explode from his chest, he would steal wallets from anyone in the room, he would build a house of cards on the back of his hands. All anyone had to do was ask. But no one did, because they were sure he would crack in the middle, fall to the floor, and leave something suspended they could never fix. So instead of magic, he sang an old Nathan McCoy song about losing something in Hawaii. He had a falsetto you could feel across your shoulders. His hands were thin, he hadn't slept in two months, and you were the only one who knew that a few weeks earlier he had parked his car somewhere and lost it. When he was too sick to come out for his own garage sale, he told you to give everything away. You watched people take his couch, his television, his doves, and you felt like you were officiating a slow robbery. *If you're a decent magician*, he once told you, *when you die people will miss you. But if you're a really great magician, they'll always think you're alive and in the middle of the best trick of all time.* Even though you watched him fade in front of a machine, heard his breathing disappear like a radio station slipping off the air, you still look for him now. In the eyes of the teller at the bank, in the stands at minor league baseball games, in the credits of independent movies from Iceland. The only way to be sure is to look everywhere.

How to Get Mail in the Suburbs

When you are twelve your sister leaves town with the mailman and the replacement guy gives everyone the wrong mail. He is tough, he wears his hat low over his eyes, and he never looks at anyone. He blares speed metal and screeches through the neighborhood. Even when you are underwater in the pool out back, you can hear him shoving letters into the boxes like he's getting back at someone for something. But no one ever complains. After he drives away, people meet in the hush of kitchens or the shadows of porches and give mail back to each other. A year before, your sister didn't tell anyone she moved in with Mark Baxter and she ruined the whole summer. Now she has ruined the neighborhood postal system. And because they can't talk about daughters or mail, your parents let you sort it out. Suddenly there are things like catalogs you know you should return to the woman next door who was Miss Texas 1967, but you are too bewitched by the silver of the world inside to do it: women on docks collecting flowers, men in great shoes riding bicycles, couples leading quiet lives on boats. At school, girls still don't like you but it doesn't keep you from falling in love with Sarah Lindsor, whose father invented an artificial valve for the heart. She took it to class for "Something I Learned About My Parents" and when she held it up it was strangely thin and small, like something that goes inside a puppet. After school, you take the long way home so you can pass by her street. The mailman there is different—he is tan and elegant and places letters in boxes as if they were made of glass. You can't remember what your old mailman looked like. Sometimes you can't remember what your sister looked like, either. The new mailman is thick and dangerous; every day he attacks the route in vicious bursts, like a slalom skier making diagonal strikes around the gates. Behind him boxes dangle off their wooden posts and vibrate meekly. He is the only person you trust.

Shark Nocturne

In July the summer turns to sharks. Signs with missing letters post warnings, but the swimmer who has been training in the open water for the Olympics decides to keep going. She has world records and she's been on the covers of magazines, but every morning when she steps off the beach into the surf, she knows none of that matters. With every stroke the waves roll drowsily over her in deep, plangent bass notes that brush against her earplugs like a distant calypso song. Underneath her the split bones of coral rise from the ocean floor like cities of drowned suburbs. Her boyfriend shows her documentaries of sharks ripping at surfers and slashing at cages, their jaws fireworks of bloody teeth, but it's no use—nothing can talk her out of the water. He has bad dreams, complains to his friends, sees a psychiatrist and then sees another one. Early in the evening when he is watering the lawn he thinks *mayday*. Above him a plane passes like a dial tone; long and luxurious, it rolls through the sky like a skimming sonance, a floating frequency, the long breath before an emergency.

Night Shift Superstar

Late at night you walk the dark surf with the girl from Huxton, the southern syrup so thick every step seems stuck to the map. She holds your hand and tells you about the Captain's boat; the fire, the silver, the sharks. How she watched the divers lower themselves into the water over the wreckage like burglars through windows in whispers. She says someone is already writing a book. It's going to be called *Throat Made of Stars*. It's been a terrible summer so far but at least everyone died quickly. Across the street at the Meseneja resort you see the nightwatchman juggling flashlights. Their beams glide through the darkness like the leftover parts of a good idea; the hiss before they fall back into his hands, a voice whispering, *California.*

Country Club Scandal

She thinks you do something special for a small startup down by the water, but you don't. You con rich guys onto the tennis court by saying you're a beginner, and in the same shorts you wore in college, play them until they lean against the fence panting. The money slips into your wallet with a faint hiss, like the warm slide of oil over a skillet. The old country club pro who taught you would be appalled, but this is how you make rent; this is how you can keep living close to the girl you love. It won't be long before headlights creep from an alley and you are chased across the parking lot and beaten up under the pier, but it doesn't matter because she loves you and because of that you're willing to get punched in the face for hours. At night she falls asleep and you stay still beside her waiting for the bats. Every night there are more. When you hear the sound of their netted press of wings fill the sky you have to keep reminding yourself it's not rain.

Rave-Ups and Galaxies

Jimmer, there's a thing in the woods and they need you. The city's gone silver, like the west coast of the moon, and it's been dusk so long they're thinking of calling it a season. After the breakup backstage, and the long, late night drive up the coast, you remember the trees on the side of the highway, twisted blasts of sculpture, old champions with bulky hands trying to find their way back to a tragedy. When you're running out of time you say everything but *I am running out of time*. You become an expert on small university basketball programs and talk about the weather at parties like you really understand it. You have to keep telling yourself to stop thinking about the girl from Huxton; it doesn't matter if she's the best kisser in the world or not. It's winter, the water is frozen, and the neighborhood cats huddle on the doorstep like French orphans from a novel. There's a thing in the woods, Jimmer. You can hear it in the hoodoo of the turbines above the highway. And we're all turning gray like we have the same fever.

One Last Wish for Claire Grogan

Late at night the deejay knows how serious it is to put a needle near anything.

Crush the Smiling Nothing

Your girlfriend broke up with you the night the Oilers won the Stanley Cup. Gretzky and Messier skated like royalty, while the other team flailed and struggled to stay standing, like third-string astronauts. Because she told her parents she was sleeping at Katie Noreyev's, and you were too far from college to drive back, after she broke up with you in the lobby, there was nothing else to do but stay together in the room you rented at the Hotel McDonald. You fought for a little while, and then things went quiet. Later, when she turned away from you in bed, you wondered if she was crying, then wondered why she wasn't. Outside you could hear the hotel in flames of celebration. The walls shook, the floors throbbed, and the streets stayed steady with currents of horns. Things were being torn apart in the name of victory and romance, and you felt stupid about the note you wrote her. Maybe quoting a dead rock star and making a weird analogy about sharks navigating their way around the world by moonlight wasn't the right way to tell her you loved her. While she slept, you opened the bottle of champagne that was chilling in a bucket by the bed and drank it yourself. It went down cold and sharp, like a world that had gone to glass, a decade turned to ice.

A Current History of Chrome

Late at night in the gym before closing there is no one left but you and two Russian gymnasts. You lift dumbbells at shaky angles, while they bring bars and plates to the ceiling as if they're writing messages in the air. One of them gets on his back, lowers a mass of weight to his chest and brings it upward. From the ceiling, the air conditioner hums a mechanical breeze and from the radio a saxophone solo slinks its way through the speakers. When he begins struggling under the weight, the bar shaking in his hands, the other leans over and whispers, *I love you.*

Emergency Anthem

When the guy with the gun ran into the restaurant she owned, stole a strawberry danish, and shot his head off in the women's bathroom, you stood around the body unsure of what to do with your hands. The man with the beard and the hat said he had known a little bit about him, told you he'd swallowed glass at a party once to prove a point. What was the point, she asked. Just chewed it up and swallowed it while everyone watched, he said. What was the point? she asked again. It's probably still in him, he said. Then the police came and did quick math around the body, all the while not looking worried, as if the seriousness of a thing depended on how long it took to clean it up. Later, she closed the restaurant and the two of you sat around the big black table in the back. She was sad about the man and you were sorry you had nothing clever to say about dying. On the news a boy broke a record by skipping a rock thirty-four times, baseball players were traded for other baseball players to be named later, and the weatherman you went to high school with said the big storm was going to be bigger than he thought. You held her hand and waited for the rain and thought about how terrible it is that we remember so much.

Song from a Bonfire

The magician's son is no good at magic. From the dock you watch another trick break weakly over his knuckles. You remember his father from those television specials in the '70s; he'd cut people in half, swallow swimming pools, sink mountains into sand. But his son is not able to sense the wave where things disappear; even matches sputter for him. But when it's night and he plays guitar on the beach around a bonfire, we form a tight circle around him. We watch the flames climb out of the darkness and feel them slowly pull the skin tight across our faces.

Winter of the Black Drum

The painter fell in the ocean, and as he sank, there was nothing he could do but marvel at the colors of the drowning world. And when he saw the tilting blue between the rocks, the green that twisted into a deep country luster, the toneless backs of currents bursting into blazes of taupe tendons, all he could think was, *I never would have thought of that.*

Kelly Crosby

Nobody understood how much you loved Kelly Crosby. You were nine and she was seventeen but you didn't see why that should matter. Summer opened up now that you knew she was in it. You confessed your love in a note to her that ended with a quote from a song about foxes. You found out where she lived and rode past her house every day, trying to look like you knew about romance. Nobody seemed to notice except the man at the top of the street who always waved because he thought you lived there. The only time you saw her, she was washing a car with a guy so handsome it made you feel like you would always be someone small on a stupid red bike. On the way home the world started to vanish and you tried to remember the fantasy where she was waiting for you under a waterfall of arrows. You never gave her the note; it went through the wash and ended up a taut ball in your pocket, the letters a faint seam slicing up the side. For the rest of the summer, the next-door neighbors sat in their hot tub without swimsuits and played country records. Boys on big bikes blew through the night. Young couples made out on car hoods. And at dusk, as the heat lowered and settled onto the street, sprinklers lisped the alphabet across shadowed lawns.

West Coast Feedback

Amy Medders moved in across the street two days after the end of eleventh grade. She was from London and looked different than the California girls whose ponytails sat in single spikes on the tops of their heads. She wore headbands and a leather jacket and had glasses that angled across her face in a slice of fashion you had never seen before. In the fall you knew everyone at school would learn quickly about her, but for now she was summer's best secret and you were going to keep her to yourself. You would teach her how to surf. You would play her records by obscure bands from Australia. But late in July her family moved to France and that was that. The orders came from men in ties standing in high rooms overlooking famous tilting cities who couldn't care less about a boy falling in love in the middle of summer. Having watched the boxes go back inside the truck, like a dream in reverse, you felt sick for weeks. September came, and as soon as school started, you stopped going; chose instead to surf Rubicon point and listen to a mix you made called "Songs From Abandoned Semesters." One day you fell and the ocean held you between its powerful forearms, dragged you across the coral, and scraped you underneath in a long, jagged drag. You felt your body go dim, your breath get lost like a shrinking signal. Then the blue tendons of the swell relaxed and raised you back into the world to start over again.

Excerpt from the Documentary
Six Famous Magicians

After the magician died, the coroner stood for hours around the body waiting for something to happen.

Air Fountain

A laugh is just as important as every hand that pulls shoulders through walls, as crucial as the angle of the wrist of the girl in black who paints portraits of squids, and just as quick as the rivers that run through the room, under the bed, and end up in a big pool of hats and ladders outside the window. I hope you come home soon; nobody else thinks I'm funny.

680 South to 680 South

She stepped over the jagged hundreds in careful diagonals, came up behind you on the pier at Surguesa and said, *It's terrible in the middle*. A few days later you saw the painter's son put a jar of ocean on her doorstep, and by the time she woke up, the two of you had fought down by the docks. Your hands were bloody, his nose was broken, and it took days for you to get the sand out of your mouth. For the remainder of the summer, passing by her window on your bike, the jar glared at you with its one good eye. The water had grown green in the sun and once you even thought you saw something moving inside. Passing by the rangers on their horses, you dared yourself to throw a rock at her window, yell something important up to her. But you knew it was too late and any chance with her had angled away from you. The night before you left, you watched the two of them head down to the water. When the clouds shifted, you saw they were kissing and her shirt was open. You turned around and all the blurry lights below you looked like the sky had reversed itself, and the stars were really buildings and houses and other people's lives. You put your hands in your pockets and walked alone into the night like someone who had lost a fortune; like someone who used to be famous.

Night Division

The girl in the black dress sat on the pier with a man who was not a doctor. They had both been doing terrible things all summer, but even from far away it was easy to tell which one knew more about the night.

Across the water The Captain held an axe in one hand and dragged something across the deck with the other. When he set the ship on fire he thought, *Nobody's going to remember me this way.*

Let the West Coast Be Settled

In the darkness of his office the doctor tells you that you'll never see orange again. At the café, when the waitress tucks her blonde hair behind her ear and smiles, you wonder if you'll even miss it. Weeks later you learn that it won't be long before the other colors loosen from the muddy riverbank behind your eyes and vanish. You wake up in a cold panic; picture your heart as a big grey engine wheezing across a withering track. One night you see a blue wolf in your backyard drinking from the fountain. When he turns to face you, you notice his eyes are the color of a sword behind ice. Summer is over; the team that was supposed to win didn't, the band that was supposed to change everything broke up, and the young actress was found dead on the beach. Even though it's only September, Halloween decorations are already up—skeletons dangle from doors and pumpkins with carved, wet mouths perch on porches. You stand in what's left of the sunlight and try to remember how many heartbeats a hummingbird gets. You look at the flowers in your garden and wonder how you'll remember them. Later, you sit in the darkness of your room and think, *Get it over with.*

With warm thanks to the following publications in which some of the work in this book previously appeared, occasionally in a different form:

Barrow Street:	"Giverny Floodlands"
The Canary:	"California Divorce"
	"Summer Job, Year Seven"
Cranky:	"Strobe Light Retrospective"
Faultline:	"Why You'll Never Live in Ithaca"
Hawaii Pacific Review:	"Song from a Bonfire"
The Nervous Breakdown:	"California Divorce"
New Ohio Review:	"Summer at Pitch 77"
	"They'll Know When You're Gone"
	"Blue Door Option"
Parthenon West Review:	"Gene Clark"
	"Tillbrook Crimes"
	"Kelly Crosby"

ABOUT THE AUTHOR

ALEX GREEN was born in California and raised in the East Bay. A two-time nominee for the Pushcart Prize in Poetry, his work has appeared in *RHINO*, *The Canary*, the *Mid-American Review*, and *Barrow Street*. He is the author of *The Stone Roses* (Bloomsbury Academic). He currently teaches at St. Mary's College of California and is the Editor of www.stereoembersmagazine.com. You can visit him at www.alexgreenbooks.com.

Alejandro Ventura, *Puerto Rico*
Alex Green, *Emergency Anthems*
Anselm Berrigan & Jonathan Allen, *LOADING*
Bill Rasmovicz, *Idiopaths*
Broc Rossell, *Unpublished Poems*
Carol Guess, *Darling Endangered*
Chris O Cook, *To Lose & to Pretend*
Christopher Hennessy, *Love-In-Idleness*
Dominique Townsend, *The Weather & Our Tempers*
Erika Jo Brown, *I'm Your Huckleberry*
Jackie Clark, *Aphoria*
Jared Harel, *The Body Double*
Jay Besemer, *Telephone*
Joanna Penn Cooper, *The Itinerant Girl's Guide to Self-Hypnosis*
Joe Fletcher, *Already It Is Dusk*
Joe Pan, *Autobiomythography & Gallery*
John F. Buckley & Martin Ott, *Poets' Guide to America*
John F. Buckley & Martin Ott, *Yankee Broadcast Network*
Joseph P. Wood, *Broken Cage*
Julia Cohen, *Collateral Light*
Lauren Russell, *Dream-Clung, Gone*
Laurie Filipelli, *Elseplace*
Martin Rock, *Dear Mark*
Matt Runkle, *The Story of How All Animals Are Equal & Other Tales*
Matt Shears, *10,000 Wallpapers*
Michelle Gil-Montero, *Attached Houses*
Noah Eli Gordon, *The Word* Kingdom *in the Word Kingdom*
Paige Taggart, *Or Replica*

BAP

Brooklyn Arts Press

Brooklyn Arts Press (BAP) is an independent house devoted to publishing poetry books, lyrical fiction, short fiction, novels, art monographs, chapbooks, translations, & nonfiction by emerging artists. We believe we serve our community best by publishing great works of varying aesthetics side by side, subverting the notion that writers & artists exist in vacuums, apart from the culture in which they reside and outside the realm & understanding of other camps & aesthetics. We believe experimentation & innovation, arriving by way of given forms or new ones, make our culture greater through diversity of perspective, opinion, expression, & spirit.

Our staff is comprised of literary loyalists whose editorial resolve, time, effort, & expertise allows us to publish the best of the manuscripts we receive.

Visit us at BrooklynArtsPress.com